# EMERGED

Te'Ann Peaker

*For my loves Mi-Lia, Elijah and Halo without ya'll this would not be possible. For my family and friends that never gave up on me. The people that made an impact in my life and never let me fall thank you! Thank you God for always having my back and allowing me to share my testimony.*

# CONTENTS

Title Page
Dedication
Foreword
Introduction
Preface

| | |
|---|---|
| SHOTS FIRED | 1 |
| TWISTED | 14 |
| TOXIC | 18 |
| HORNS | 22 |
| THE SCARE | 30 |
| UNWILLING | 34 |
| LOVE LOST | 36 |
| COVER-UP | 39 |
| HEARTACHE | 43 |
| BREAKING POINT | 47 |
| HEALING | 51 |
| Afterword | 53 |
| About The Author | 55 |

# FOREWORD

*Everyone at some point in their lives, has an idea or a picture in their minds how they want their lives to be. Whether it is when we were little children, or as adults dreaming of a better life we all had those thoughts and dreams come into our minds.*

*Unfortunately, the reality is that those dreams and ideas don't always turn out the way that we had played them out in our heads. In this riveting book, Te'Ann shows the true resilience of a person who faces the bitterness of a tainted reality and the sweetness of realizing purpose through pain. There's one part of her story that I remember receiving the devastating news and praying for her miracle. Those prayers paid off. Although life and time caused us to lose touch, the connection of care and compassion was never lost.*

*There are peaks and valleys along this thing called life but the most important thing is to learn lessons to help other's along the journey. This book takes us on a roller coaster journey of emotions, persistence, heartache, restoration and self realization. This book shows us that we can continue to have dreams and goals. We should not stop moving forward towards divine purpose. This book is a gateway to re-birthing and restoration! The next chapters of Te'Ann's life will be filled with God's guidance, purpose and her resilience to keep on moving towards the greatness that lives within her!*

Chelsealya "Cookie" Payne

# INTRODUCTION

*It's amazing how life is unpredictable, in my book I share my testimonies and the struggles that almost ended my life. In life you never consider the consequences that can result from your actions or even other's. Learning is a process, either you grow from it or you will stay at a stand still. I made decisions that caused me pain and other's as well. It's what you take from your mistakes that makes life worth living for. It's not about what people think of you but it's about you loving yourself in the mist of everything. I had to take pieces of my life to be able to acknowledge the woman I am today and healing from the hurt is how I broke free. Just know love does not lie, abuse, curse, destroy you but it builds the person within you. If you take anything from my story please understand that life is a gift and every moment is precious.*

# PREFACE

*All the events that are recorded in this book are my truth and my personal experiences. I need to share my story, hoping it saves someone's life or give them the strength to keep fighting no matter what my occur in life.*

# SHOTS FIRED

*In June of 2000 my life was drastically changed. I woke up one summer morning not realizing my world was about to be turned upside down. Just two days prior, my aunt had warned me about a recent dream. The look in her eyes was so intense and concerning it captured my full attention. She proceeded to tell me her dream, stating that I had been shot and I was lying helplessly in the alley behind my grandmother's house bleeding. I was thinking yeah right, that cannot happen to me. However, her dream, in part, soon became my reality.*

*The neighborhood that I chose to hang out in was a known drug zone with a murderous past. I knew inside that it wasn't the best place for me to be and I should have listened to friends and family who had tried to deter me from hanging out in that area. I desperately needed and wanted to get away from my family at times because I felt like I just didn't belong. At times I would actually wonder if I had been adopted; perhaps I just wished I had been.*

*Life has so many turning points. During January 2000 I meet this handsome guy. He was hood, chocolate with dimples and he had a very nice build. He was also a drug dealer. I had never been with someone that was in the streets so heavy. Not long after we started hanging out I started doing things that I knew were out of character and wrong but I didn't care. It was all new and exciting for me. My life was doing a 360 degree turn, I started smoking cigarettes and weed, going on runs with him and even holding his products. The police got to know me very well through my association with him and they would tell me to find something stable because my situation was temporary.*

*This guy and I were like a team minus the killing, bank robberies; folks called us TNT like dynamite. We were Bonnie and Clyde around our county. I stopped caring about certain things and my attitude worsened. We would fight other people together on a regular basis but things changed almost suddenly when he redirected all his animosity toward me and started hitting on me. When they say love is blind it really is, I thought well if he is hitting me that means he loves me or he at least cares.*

*Soon after in February of that year I was charged with possession of marijuana, concealing a deadly weapon and possession of controlled substances.*

*Those were, my first charges. I was arrested and at the time I had a large sum of money in my possession. I spent six deafening hours in a cell for the man that I thought cared for me. I felt like my arrest and charges would prove my loyalty to him. At the time my dad worked for the police department so they immediately called him and informed him of my situation. I felt so embarrassed, I practically begged the officer not to open my cell door because I knew if they opened that gate he was going to beat my ass. While all this was going on I had drugs concealed but, they didn't do a cavity check to my relief. The officer transported me to the county jail where I was processed and booked. The worst feeling was not knowing what the outcome would be. I hadn't been in trouble before, I was afraid that the police would use me to get to my boyfriend at the time. Eventually, I was released from that hell hole on my own recognizance with future court dates that would determine my future. As I exited the county jail there my boyfriend was waiting patiently. When the gates finally opened, there were no hugs, no kisses, no concerns. He simply wanted to know if the police had taken the money. My heart was crushed, even though I thought he only cared about the money, I still loved him. Honestly I was just happy to be out of that hell hole.*

*I remember thinking that I would have to come up with money for a lawyer and explain what had occurred to my family first thing in the morning I thought that taking the charge for him would prove my loyalty, but all it did was make me his punching bag. I used to wake up in the morning barely able to open my eyes, chest hurting and teeth hurting from being punched in the mouth. I thought that was love, I didn't know any better to think any different but I knew I loved him. In April of that year he got locked up. Oh my god my heart fell out of my chest and I'm like what am I going to do now. I immediately came up with a plan and put it into action. I knew he needed a lawyer so I started to sell his product to get money so that I would be able hold him down. So once again I put my life and freedom on the line to show him how down I was for him, not realizing how far in the streets I was headed. I started making plays so he could have money on his books, while in lockup. I would go see him faithfully; I was missing my chocolate. Without second guessing it I stayed in the streets the entire time he was away, smoking weed, selling drugs to put on his book and making sure he had clothes when he got home from jail. I got buck-wild in the streets. My family wouldn't see me for weeks at a time. I did not know if I was punishing them or myself.*

*One night everything caught up with me, I had just finished smoking some weed with some of my associates, and I decided to go home after being away for days. On the way my friend got a call and we got turned around because my jailed boyfriend wanted to talk, so we headed in another direction. We were only a few minutes from her this cousin's house when somebody we knew flagged us down. Not knowing what was going on, my friend stopped the car to talk. Suddenly another guy we knew frantically jumped in the backseat of the vehicle stating that he needed to go to the store right away. My friend refused and demanded that he get out of her car. At that time a third man approached the passenger side of the vehicle where I was sitting. He peered into the vehicle. I knew him as well. That's the moment my life changed. I looked back again and noticed that the guy that came to the passenger window had a loaded 38 handgun in his grip and he started shooting into the backseat where the male passenger was sitting. I didn't know what to do, my heart and mind instantly began racing. I glanced over at the driver she was screaming with her face pressed against the steering wheel. That's when I decided to put my head in between my legs to escape the gunfire. That didn't do me any good, I had been struck in my neck and face multiple times. The sensation of that hot metal burning through my flesh and fracturing my jaw bone remains unforgettable. At that moment my aunt's dream was no longer a dream, it had just become my reality. All I could think is God please don't let me die, I'm sorry for everything I've ever done "please don't let me die", as the shooter finished unloading bullets into the car. I removed my jacket and wrapped it around my neck to apply pressure until we got some help. I felt my teeth loosening inside of my mouth and pieces of bone from my jaw. Blood was everywhere.*

*I patiently waited to tell everyone in the vehicle I had*

been shot, mainly because I didn't want the shooter to realize he had shot the wrong person and decide to kill all of us to avoid witnesses. The driver finally was able to get up the courage to pull off. I firmly believed that the guy in the backseat was dead, there was no way he was alive after all of that. At this point is when I finally let everyone in the car know that I was shot. The guy in the back quickly responded saying "I can't believe he shot you." I couldn't understand how everyone else in the car escaped unscathed as the battle for my life was about to begin. We began to make our way to the police station which was about five minutes from where the shooting occurred. When we suddenly realized the tires had been shot out, forcing us to stop and request for someone to call the paramedics. My friend and the guy in the back seat immediately hopped out of the car and began banging on each and every door in an attempt to seek out aid for me. Everything suddenly got seemingly quiet and I clearly heard a still small voice instruct me to go to the house nearest me. As I followed these instructions I made sure I continuously applied pressure to my wounds and securely placed my identification in my back pants pocket and proceeded to a house directly on the corner. I knocked on the door and a couple answered. Shocked at what they were observing, they frantically began asking questions about what happened. Who did this to you, they asked. I couldn't respond. The couple was caring enough to invite me inside of their home until help arrived. However, I refused their offer because I didn't want to ruin their carpet and furniture with blood. So instead I sat on the steps at the entrance of *their home patiently waiting, when my friend arrived with an off duty paramedic. He visually inspected me and simply stated "I can't believe you're able to talk." Due to the bullet striking my tongue blood was literally pouring out of my mouth as I was talking. The paramedic informed me that my wounds were fractions of an Inch away from my major arteries. In my head all I could do was thank God. Since my injuries were so severe I was airlifted to Maryland shock trauma unit. I remember the helicopter ride like it was yesterday, I didn't want to die, my life had just started. I have heard people that had near death experience see their life flash before their eyes, but I can truly say that didn't happen to me. I was completely alert, conversing with the paramedic in the helicopter. I even recall singing Tupac in my head "Me and my girlfriend." Finally I remember landing on the roof of the hospital, being taken out of the helicopter, and the emergency team rushing me into the hospital. It felt like I was in a movie that I had seen before. The doctors were asking me questions about my health, the location of the pain, and the level of pain. I remember making them laugh, despite my dire situation. I don't recall much else. I was taken into surgery.*

*Post surgery as the anesthesia began to wear off I remember seeing my dad, aunt, uncle, and grandmother. All I could do was cry because I truly felt that as if I disappointed them in so many ways. However, I was alive to make things right. Surgeons had inserted a trachea, and wired my mouth shut* due as I had a fractured jaw. I learned that the bullets I was shot with was hollow tips. Tubes were placed in my nasal passages to allow a path for oxygen. I couldn't talk, I had to write everything down. The doctors said I was going to need a speech therapist to learn how to speak again. I didn't want to look at myself, I didn't even feel beautiful or recognize my face. When I would stand up my head would go to one side. The emergency room team didn't want me to get up because I could hurt myself but that didn't stop me. I went from one hundred and forty-nine pounds to ninety-nine pounds within a few days. I had nightmares at night thinking that the shooter would come back to finish the job due to media outlets putting my name and street address in the press. I pushed myself to get better, I would get up and walk around the hospital to get my strength back. My younger brother came from Georgia to take care of me. He would spend the night with me because I was afraid, but he really made me feel safe. The nurses would come in the room and say things like "hello beautiful," and all I could do was wonder what the hell they were looking at while they were speaking to me. My friends would call me out of concern, knowing that I couldn't talk. I would respond by simply pressing the phone buttons to let them know that I heard them. I remained in the shock trauma unit for a week; I was determined to get back home. I'm a fighter and I don't know what it is to give up.

The word on the street was that my face had been

blown off, that I was disfigured and even worse that I had died.

I was in a depressed state of mind and I knew that I had to get out of it, even though I was weak. I was determined to to normal, when I went home. After getting home, I still felt like an outcast after all that had occurred. My grandmother was the primary one taking care of me. She really didn't know how to express affection and be compassionate, because of the way she had been raised, which resulted in negative degrading comments. My trachea needed constant cleaning and I was fed through a feeding tube that was routed through my nose to my stomach due to the facial injuries. I recall my aunt's fiancé prepared a Jamaican steak dish, pureed it, and forced it through a syringe into the feeding tube for me. Although I appreciated it my taste buds were nonexistent. I survived on vanilla flavored supplement drinks for a while. I couldn't sleep at night so I would stay up watching television and I would rest during the day. I felt safer sleeping while others were awake around me because I was in constant worry about my safety. On the outside I felt very ugly with what had happened to my face; I wondered if I had done something awful to deserve what had happened to me.

The perpetrator who nearly took my life had been apprehended and I had to get myself prepared for court. I believed in my heart that at some point and time I would forgive him for what he had done to me.

The next few months were very hard for me as I tried to regain my self-esteem. Eventually things started to go as planned, the feeding tube came out my nose, the wires were taken off and then the trachea was removed. My jaw was very sore, the doctors stated I would need speech therapy but God knew better.

Months later the court date came up in October, the perpetrator who shot me got life plus seventeen years. I forgave him for almost ending my life and that gave me the strength to move on.

One night my home girl called asking if I wanted to go out. I agreed, although I knew damn well I didn't need to go anywhere but I was bored from being in the house. I went out, like an idiot, and it didn't go well. On the way home from the club, her car stopped and she got out to see what was going on. A familiar still voice told me to get out of the car. I questioned that voice for a second, but I remembered that voice coming to me when I got shot. I listened to that voice a second time, as soon as I got out the car it caught on fire from front to back and I was wondered what the hell was going on, must must have nine lives? An old school van pulled up with tinted windows. No one emerged from the van to ask if my homegirls and

*I needed help. My friend walked towards the van, I told her that she was crazy, because people could try to snatch us. I started walking to the traffic light thinking I'll be damned if they get me. I should have kept my butt at home. We began to hear sirens, the van drove off and I was thanking God once again. Meantime I tried to stuff my friend's mouth full of french fries because she had been drinking at the club. My dad was the one who showed up on the scene to take me home. All I could do is sit there in silence. Once again, I had experienced another near death experience which ultimately led me to decide to get a full time job, use my time constructively and most importantly not die of boredom.*


*Life hasn't been easy for me, it seems to get worse at times and I try to find my destiny in life. At times I feel like I'm a failure mostly everyday I wake up. I'm a single mother trying daily to make ends meet but I do not know if I'm a good mother anymore. I fight for them, I need for their life to be better than mine has been thus far. There are a lot of factors in life that I have complete control over, yet in other instances things are completely out of my control and usually result in the worst possible things happening. Periodically, I wonder why I'm still breathing because I have been hurting most of my life, looking for love in all the wrong men. Feeling unloved by your family could potentially make anyone drift off with the wrong people. I have learned a lot of things that I do not want for myself as a result of drifting off. I do not want to be stuck in the same place in life. I have* achieved a few of my goals and that's something that let's me know I can make it. I have cried plenty of nights and asked God the question "why me?" When my peers see me they see someone strong, but I don't feel that way. I am a person that has been hurting for most of my life. Sometimes I don't even think God is listening to me because I keep having heartaches. All I know I need to make a positive impact on the world. I know I have some type of purpose in life, I just don't know where to begin. People tell me that I have a testimony. I feel my life won't be at peace until I release the hurt that has been bottled up within me for years now. As a child I wanted to be loved beyond measure and I needed that love especially from my dad. As my father's only daughter, I felt like he did not want to protect his little girl, nor did he even care. I never admitted to anyone that my jumping between relationships had something to do with not having a dad to teach me how a man is supposed to treat a woman. I always felt like if my father would have been engaged in my life that certain people would have never gotten into my inner circle; I have always felt vulnerable in that regard. I always felt like something in my life is missing; somehow, I want to blame my dad for all the bad men in my life. However, I really cannot do that, because I have seen red flags from the beginning. I have tried try to figure out ways to move on from my past but something always reminds me of the pain.

EMERGED

# TWISTED

*About a year after I got shot my ex returned from jail. I used to visit him with my trachea, feeding tube and wired jaw. Things had gotten rough before he was locked up, but I thought he would change especially after he had seen me broken. The abuse, cheating, lying and getting back in the streets started all over again. I remember him choking me at times until I blacked out. I would beg for my life all the time, but I still stayed with him. I didn't know how to walk away from him. My grandmother liked him. I remember vividly them two sitting on the bed and my grandmother showing him a life insurance policy on me. I never understood how she could do something like that to me as her granddaughter. I believed that he would respect my loyalty to after I had been shot and took a charge for him. However, the beatings started getting worse. He also cheated on me several times. Eventually I decided to walk away from the relationship because it was causing me to be depressed. To free my mind and spirit I decided to meet someone new.*

My new beau eventually came to my grandma's house to spend some time with me, he was really cute. He was something different, not a hood guy. The new relationship went downhill quickly when my ex boyfriend found out that I had a new guy over at my grandma's house. A yellow taxi cab pulled up, I seen my ex and others jump out of the cab. I ran in the house to call the police, he kept beating on the door shouting "bitch open the door!" By the time the police arrived my ex had rode off. That's when I said enough is enough, I got tired of fighting for my life every time his hands found themselves wrapped around my throat and I didn't want to die. In early autumn I found out I was pregnant with my ex's baby. Things immediately changed for me, some folks wanted me to get an abortion, but it was my baby. I thought maybe my ex would change his abusiveness due to the pregnancy; however, that didn't change one punch after the next I hid from him at times because my main priority was to keep my baby safe. I remember I couldn't even go out without looking over my shoulder. I would always lock the car doors when I rode with other people and hold the cigarette lighter pushed in the car just in case my ex popped up. Hell he did that a lot, so I always had to be alert and on guard. A few months into my pregnancy he went back to jail, and that gave me room to breath. I used to sit and cry while thinking about the black eyes that he had given me while I carried his first child. I really wanted us to be a normal family. I didn't want my child to grow up without a father and I prayed to God that he would become a better man when he was *released.*

I landed myself a job at a warehouse making a little money. I had set my heart to buy everything that was needed for my baby. I didn't want to depend on anyone else. Working did not provide me with all the money I needed so I had a side hustle for a while. At seven months pregnant, my ex was released from jail. Although he had money when he came home, I bought him clothes. None of that even mattered, because two days later he was in a hotel room with some underage female. She called me to inform me what he was doing. I found myself angry and hurt, so I bleached all his clothes and put poison ivy in his underwear for cheating. I had no regrets. That summer I gave birth to a beautiful baby girl, which was the best feeling in the world. At that point the abuse I had suffered didn't matter much. Once again I gave my ex one last shot to get it right for our family. One day my child's father and I got into an altercation one morning. It could have turned really bad, he punched me in my face with our daughter in my arms and that became a turning point in my life. I called the police, and my dad had him removed from my grandmother's home. The officer asked me if I wanted to press chargers and I didn't. I was told that if the police had to come back for a domestic disturbance that my ex and I would both be arrested. I needed to start loving myself and stop taking the abuse!

EMERGED

# TOXIC

*When I was getting fed up with my abuser and the toxic relationship, I met this guy that swept me off my feet. He was different but I would later regret meeting him as time goes on. Initially he supported me when my ex was trying to kill me, I looked at him as a potential best friend and he had my back I believed. I felt so safe with him, in my heart I couldn't even explain it but I knew it was different. He took care of my child like my child was his and I needed that in my life. I saw the red flags, like most women I ignored them because I didn't want to see anything different. One Friday night I had got a hotel room to celebrate my homegirl's birthday, I had a babysitter so I could go to the club and everything went smoothly. I thought my guy and I were in for a romantic evening when all of sudden I heard this loud bang at the door, my heart dropped and I automatically knew it was my ex. I called downstairs for security to come up and it seemed like it took forever. As I passed the room door to go and hide in the bathroom until help came, I saw my ex through the crack of the door with a gun in his hand. He was yelling obscenities and threatening to kill me. I was thankful that he couldn't get in the room, my guy at the time was scared as hell probably wondering what he'd gotten himself into. I guess my ex had ran off by the time security arrived. My heart was beating out of my chest because this time he had been brandishing a deadly weapon. My father got involved and threatened my ex for his actions and threats against me, he was angry. I was able to view security footage with my dad. The footage showed my ex getting out of a car with the gun wrapped in a towel walking down the hotel hallway, it sent chills through me. I believed he would have killed me, the mother of his only child, he had no love for us! Through that rough weekend my man stood by me and I felt myself falling for him more. That Sunday I went back to my grandma's house to let her know what had happened but to my surprise my ex had gotten to her first. He had told my grandma over the phone that he wanted his family back with fake ass tears. I believed my grandma was going to set him straight and cuss him straight off the phone but she never did. I remembered she liked him a whole lot and I just could not understand that crap. I got into a big argument at that moment with my grandmother due to her not understanding that I didn't want to be around my ex at all. I phoned my dad and went to stay with him for a couple of days which was a relief because I was tired of fighting with my grandma and my ex. As I started to walk down the street towards my neighbors, where my dad would meet me pushing the stroller, my ex jumped out of car and began chasing me, my heart dropped. I headed back to my grandma's house and banged on the door. My grandma stuck her head out the window instead of opening the door, I just left my baby girl in her stroller on the front porch. I ran like my life depended on it, somehow my ex caught me with his hands around my neck, I found myself fighting for air but I wasn't going to just take it so I kicked him in the balls. He let go, trying to catch my breath I ran to the neighbors house to get some help and of course my ex followed me inside of the house. I was really scared for my life, I thought about my baby girl growing up without a mom. I was able to convince my ex to let me call my aunt to check on my baby. However, I called my dad and in that moment he knew something was wrong and asked if my ex was there, I replied "yes." I knew help was coming, I think he felt it too because he jumped his ass up to run out the door. I went outside because I heard police cars at my grandma's house, to my surprise it was like ten police cars out front, then my ex ran right pass me. My dad found him and left him in a fetal position. The next day my dad took me to the commissioner's office to get a restraining order because at this point I had enough and either it was his life or mine. I stayed with my dad for a while before my ex started harassing me at my dad's house. My ex had the nerve to tell my dad that I belonged to him and my dad laughed and told him that he had it wrong. There were many nights when my dad had to work, so I was left alone, that was scary. I know one thing my dad told me if he comes to his door, shoot through it and make no mistake that's exactly what I had intended to do. A few days later my ex was picked up on a warrant and ended up doing twelve years.*

EMERGED

# HORNS

*I was in a position to move on with my life, my boyfriend and I moved to Georgia after getting married. He wanted us to go to Memphis, TN with his family but I didn't want to take my baby girl with me because I didn't know how it was going to be in that environment. My mom said that we could come to her home, but we would have to be married. We were married South Carolina at my cousin's house and with a notary. We stayed there for a few weeks before heading to Atlanta. I thought everything would be okay when we got there, I was married and that is honorable. I realized sometimes the devil can be in the one you love, that was one of my lessons learned in life early and having a good heart could get you killed. I fell in love with another monster, the verbal abuse rose up, the insecurity started and it was directed at my family. My husband became really jealous of me spending time with my little brothers. I remember one night my brother asked me to do his hair and I did. When I got done I went in the room to get ready for bed, the door shut behind me and that's when I felt a hard fist on the back of my neck. I really thought I was dreaming because the pain was so* unreal, I got a back hand to the eye, I just balled up not making a sound because he would say "you don't want me to go to jail do you?" I was really embarrassed to speak-out, I made him out to be a prince, (his crazy ass) and I was wearing makeup to cover the marks on my face. At this point I really started believing maybe I deserve this abuse and that my destiny in life was getting my ass beat. I knew I couldn't allow my two youngest brothers or my child see me getting beat up. One day I got the courage to tell my mom what was going on, she informed my older brother and step dad and they made him leave. The day after I received calls from him telling me he was really sorry and that it wouldn't happen again. Knowing that I just got out of a situation dealing with abuse, he knew everything that I had dealt with that ex of mine, maybe I could forgive him this time and it will get better. We planned for me to make a trip to Memphis, Tennessee to visit him, to see if we can get the marriage back on track, we were husband and wife after all. I bought a bus ticket, got my daughter settled in to stay with my mom and stepfather while I ventured off to try to save my marriage. I knew that I wasn't taking my daughter with me. If I needed to get out, it'd be easier to do alone! Well I got my happy ass on that bus and so many thoughts were going through my head. I was trying to really think positive but when I got off the bus reality hit. I heard him say "I'm going to whoop your ass!" I should have known that was coming, I tried to show him I loved him dearly and would do anything to make it better. It's like I was signing my own death certificate thinking to myself how damn *dumb could I be, but I was a sucker for love. When I awoke the next morning he was just staring at me, a punch to head followed. The visit was only supposed to be for a week, it ended up being over a month and I was beaten everyday that I was there. We were living in an abandoned house with no water, and lights that were on only due to him stealing from someone else's home. That was not how I was use to living, hell I my ass stayed washed daily. I would get my head banged against the wall for even talking about taking a shower or about talking to my family. It was like I was his prisoner, he was my master, sometimes I would tell myself to wake the hell up from this nightmare or get the hell out of there. I knew I wasn't going to see my child if I didn't get away from him, I never felt deaths close before, but in this situation I did. One day we went to Walmart to return something because he needed gas. I left the receipt by accident on the blow up mattress that we slept on and he whooped my ass for mistakenly leaving it. That was the first time I met the devil. I wasn't high, drunk or anything and I literally saw a horn rise from his forehead. The spirit of death was embodied by him and I had to come up with a plan to remove myself from his presence for good. The next day he left me in his mom's house for a little while, so I took the opportunity to call my family because he wouldn't let me when I was around him. When I called my grandmother's house my auntie answered, she asked me if I was okay and she had to talk to me about something, she asked if I was alone and I told her yes for a little while. My aunt started to go into details about her hearing a mother give a testimony* about her daughter being held hostage by a man that she knew. She stated after the church service was over she went over to talk to the lady and her daughter. Come to find out the guy that held the lady's daughter hostage was the same one that was whooping my ass and my family was very concerned for my safety. I had gotten myself into a relationship with another crazy ass man. My mind was racing but I had to get out alive. My aunt, grandmother and I came up with a plan; they got me a bus ticket then it was all up to me after that. The next day I went through something that I knew was not normal for a person to do to another human, he woke me up out of my sleep and assaulted me sexually with objects, he wanted to inflict physical, mental and sexual pain on me. I felt so low and all I could think about was my plan to get away from that demon. We went to Walmart after all of that bullshit, and that's when I saw the devil himself; I saw horns develop from his big sweaty ass forehead. All I felt was death, I didn't even feel that when I was shot in the face and that's when I understood that God sends you warning before destruction. He punched me in my face for forgetting a damn receipt because his broke ass needed to return something for gas money. I knew I had to put my plan into effect ASAP, so I came up with some ideas that would get me out of here alive. The next day we went to the basketball court for him to catch up with some of his people. I didn't want to go because I knew other guys were going to be there and that equalled trouble for me. I'm a cute girl so you know the guys had their eyes on me when I stepped out of the car but I stayed close to the nut *because I didn't want him to think about anything. I made sure I sat on his lap the whole time, I saw him looking at me to see if my eyes were wondering but in my mind I knew I was with a crazy ass bastard. After an hour or two we left the basketball court. He questioned me asking if I remembered some guy at the court, I told him no and he pulled over and started beating me. I had scratches all over my face, blood coming out of my mouth, he told me that we were going to his mother's house and to fix my face. I wasn't putting on no damn make-up. I wanted his mom to see what kind of spineless man she had raised; but she didn't even care, she just sat there looking at me like I was crazy. I just wanted her to intervene, but it was useless. I needed to save all of my energy to get the hell out of there. The day finally came I had everything planned out, I put my child's picture on my back pocket it was my reminder on where my strength comes from. I was able to call my family letting them know the plan. My grandma bought me a bus ticket and my aunt sent me some money Western Union. I had to come up with something believable so he would take me to pick up the money so I could escape. It was tough at first because I had to keep a straight face, I was nervous, my palms were sweaty and my head started hurting like crazy. As I tried to put my thoughts in order, I told him that my family had sent some money so we could get a place. At that moment he looked at me like yeah right, but for some reason he thought I was telling the truth. We got in the car and headed to the nearest Western Union which ended up being in a Kroger grocery store. He sat in the car while I headed into the store. When I got inside the store I took my child's picture out of my back pocket to kiss it because there was no turning back! I approached one of the store's security guards to let him know I was being held against my will, tears started to roll down my face as he called the manager of the store. I explained the whole situation I was in with a few short words, the manager looked at me and told me to stop crying because everything would work out. In the meantime, he took his time at the Western Union counter to give the police time to pull up. I was a nervous wreck as I tried to keep it together, and my face was hurting from the blows the day before. I was too ready to get away from his crazy ass. He came into the store stating that the security came up to him to inform him somebody didn't want him here and I'm tried to play it off by going to the manager and asked if there was a problem. I was scared but the manager went along with me and told him that what he had said wasn't true. I believe he was just testing the waters. He kept looking at me asking what's wrong. I looked like I was crying and I told him that I was just tired. I didn't want to give it away, I wanted to say you crazy MF I'm getting the hell out of here but I had to keep the game face. Even though I knew I was getting out of there, I started to get emotional so I went to the bathroom to pull it together. Not even four seconds later the manager came into the bathroom letting me know the police had arrived and they had him in custody. Who would have known he had a warrant from an incident that happened a few years prior. I hopped in a cab an headed to the bus station, my heart was still racing, I* was scared as hell but I was headed to peace and excited to see my child. There was a line at the bus station, an then an announcement over the intercom that another bus was needed because they had reached capacity. My heart fell out of my chest, I was like you gotta be kidding me, almost to freedom and thenI looked up and saw three police officers. They walked over to me and stated that my family called them to make sure I got on that bus safely. I told the officers that the bus was full going to Atlanta and they were sending another one. The police officer looked at me and said you're getting on that bus, he took me to the front of the line letting them know enough to get me on that bus. Ten minutes later I was pulling out heading to my destination and I haven't looked back since.

The twisted part about the whole thing is that the demon that I had married had taken another female hostage back in another state. The other female was in the armed forces and was the daughter of a lady that went to church with my aunt. He had the other female locked in a room. She and I actually talked when entire ordeal was over. She informed me that she could hear my then boyfriend and I together. He had her locked in a room, and she was AWOL as a result. I remembered asking him what was in the back room and he had directed me not to go in that room because it was full of crap, I didn't ever think too much about it and didn't ask any further questions. I wish I would have known sooner we could have both escaped the madness and abuse. I'm *just thankful God allowed me another chance at life and a safe return to my child.*

# THE SCARE

*I don't really believe in people that can look into the future but one particular time I decided to try one.* One day I was talking to my cousin, and she told me that she had been talking to this older lady that could supposedly tell me what's going on in my life and I decided to take her up on it. What I learned almost turned my life upside down. Basically, she told me that my child's father had been sleeping with an escort who was HIV positive. I knew he was messing with a woman that was an escort, because he was her personal driver and partially that was a reason why I ended our relationship. I needed to get tested right away, so the following week I went to a nearby clinic where they do HIV swab tests on the spot. I took my two little ones with me because I was really worried, I just had a baby five months prior and all my blood work was fine during that time. A staff member explained the process, and swabbed the inside of my cheeks. The waiting began, my heart was racing, my mind was imagining my life with this disease if it came back positive. God knows I have been through so much in my life, I was only twenty-four years old and I had dealt with things the average person doesn't go through. Well this time it was two medical staff members that entered the room to give me the news. I just held on to my kids so tight, thinking no matter what they will still love me unconditionally. I was told me I was HIV positive, I cried and didn't know what to feel or how to feel at that moment. I was trying to be strong for my kids because I have been that way for so long, I didn't want them to worry about me. I called my mother to inform her about my results, I could hear the hurt in her voice and she couldn't believe it. That's the first time I had ever experienced crying with my mother and stated you have been through so much Tee. I pulled it together enough to pack my kids up to leave and they didn't say we need to run further tests to make sure. They let me just walk out the door with no type of sympathy, I was lost like how could my ex do this to me and my babies, I loved my ex but how could he lay down with me knowing he had been with someone with HIV damn! I called him as soon as I got home and yelled at him as I told him the news. He stated that it was impossible and that he would get a blood test to be sure. I didn't want to live at that point, because I didn't know how my life would turn out. I realize things happen in life but wondered why these things happened to me. I believed that I was a good person with a loving heart and I just didn't understand. My mind was all over the place, I decided I was going to end my life, I headed towards the spaghetti junction by Gwinnett County, Georgia to go over the bridge. The sad part about it is I had my two kids in the car, I was working up the nerves to end my life. When my phone rang and it was my mom *and my step dad telling me to come to them. They told me that God was in control and not to claim anything. Something clicked in my head, I had to put my faith in God. All I did was cry, I prayed so much. I would throw up, I couldn't eat, sleep or even get out of bed. My aunt called me to explain that many things could give that test a positive response, my mom paid for me to go to the doctors to get a blood test. I went one Thursday morning, I couldn't eat, sleep, I could barely breathe and I just patiently waited until I was called to the back. Palms are sweaty, it felt like it was a hundred degrees in that damn doctors office, it was either run the hell out of that office or put my faith in the man upstairs. I was being called to have my blood drawn. With the easy part was over, the worrying started all over again. My mother and stepfather decided we should take a trip because it was Memorial Day weekend. It was going to be a long wait for those test results, I guess they wanted me to take my mind off it for a few days. I couldn't function properly half of the time. We returned back to Atlanta the day after Memorial Day weekend. I didn't want to call the doctor's office by myself so I phoned my uncle and we proceeded to ring the doctor's office but not without praying first. The phone line started to ring, the nurse picked up, I stated I was inquiring about my HIV test and learned that everything came back negative. So many tears ran down my face, thank you God! I learned a lot through that whole process and I knew that God had brought me too far to turn away now. My family prayed for me and there is nothing like the power of prayer.*

EMERGED

# UNWILLING

When you're a single mother sometimes you have put a hustle into play when your children need something and that's what I thought I was doing. One day I went to my homegirls house to get my daughters hair braided and that's when I came across the island guy. He had the longest dreads I ever seen at that time. He stated he would pay someone to do his hair and of course I volunteered. Hell I needed the money. I was supposed to do his hair at my homegirls place but she had gotten sick so plans changed. I went over later on that Sunday afternoon, my son had just been dropped off and I put him in my room to finish his nap. When island guy came in I felt like something wasn't right but I proceeded to sit on the couch, while he sat on the floor. Everything was going as planned until he started talking sexual to me. The next thing I knew I was being chased around the coffee table. It was like a grizzly chasing a deer, I didn't want to panic and wake up my son from sleeping because I didn't need him to witness anything that was going on in that moment. I just laid there thinking why is this happening, did I do something wrong and how will this end. After it was finished he got up smiling saying nobody has to know, I felt like trash and violated. How does trying to make money to support your kids turn into an experience from hell. When he walked out my front door, I just hit the ground with tears rolling down my face. I know I needed to let someone know what happened, especially not knowing if he would come back. I didn't want to call the police because I was embarrassed and how could I let this man into my home. I just dealt with it, buried it in the back of my head and continued on with my life. Nevertheless I do think about it from time to time but I didn't let it break me.

# LOVE LOST

*I was a mother of two children at the time and I was doing my best for them. I did have financial help from my family but I still was craving something in my lonely life. When I was fifteen years old my mom remarried, that was the beginning and ending of my life for me. I wasn't a perfect child, I did a lot of sneaky stuff behind my mother's back, I didn't like school because I always got picked on. Don't get me wrong, my mother did the best she could but when it came to men she would put them before her kids. My new stepdad overstepped his boundaries with us and she let him. He would beat my brother, talk crazy to me but we were kids. It was always us three making it happen, my brother and I fought a lot but hey every sibling has their moments. We stuck together no matter what, and I never that a new man coming into the family would've changed our bond but it did. I started seeing this older guy looking for love that I wasn't getting at home. I didn't really know any better, I thought he really cared about me and I decided to mess with him. Well one day I had my older guy come pick me up for a few hours but I didn't return home the same way I left. I walked in the* house with my lips looking like I got kicked in my mouth but I had let my Morehouse guy suck on them. It was so damn embarrassing, I tried to lie to my mom about it because I didn't want her to find out about him. Man when she did, she called the college to talk to the dean and that was the end of my life. I was sent to live with my grandma, I felt that my mom didn't want me anymore and she was making a new life with her husband. I didn't want to leave her or my brother, we were always together. My heart never felt the same after that and I felt that my life went to shit. I just felt like everyone was throwing me away, my dad didn't want anything to do with me and now my mom put me on the back burner. Why was I brought into this world to be unloved, God why me and will they ever love me. It's hard going through life feeling unwanted by the ones that are automatically supposed to love you. So many nights I cried wondering what's wrong with me. I know I wasn't the perfect child, maybe that had a negative stain on my relationships but I still needed that love in my life. My mom never told me why I shouldn't do things and that made me curious. Like most girls, I wanted a normal life but I received nothing but that. Don't get me wrong my mom did the best she could being a single mother, with no help from our father's and when I was younger I remember her always providing. I used to dream that I was adopted, I always felt like I didn't belong and why was I even here. When I started having children, I had to do the opposite and that allowed me to love again. No parent is perfect at no point but I promised my kids I wouldn't ever give up on them. It's been a struggle *and it's well worth it.*

# COVER-UP

*I had already been married twice at this point and why not do it a third time. Hell they say the third time's a charm but I doubt it. I reconnected with an old flame from my street running days, we started conversing again once we got older but should have left him a past fling. Well things went well for about six months before we decided to get married, his boss paid for the wedding and all I had to do was get my dress. We brought our rings, he got the marriage license and all we had to do is get hitched. Everything was set for the green light, in the spring we were married. My married name had a nice ring to it. I left Georgia to be with my husband and lived in his parents house initially living with his parents wasn't a piece of cake, they were too holy for my blood and they forgot they were once human. I believe those are the worst type of Christians, they are self righteous, perhaps they just wanted to put their sorry ass son on me. They had custody of their grandson son from a previous relationship, so they felt like they could control his life and he let them. After a few months things started going down hill and it was time for us to find a place. It got really overwhelming going back from his parents house to my grandma's place. Sometimes my kids and I would sleep in my van my grandmother purchased for me because we had nowhere else to sleep. I was getting very depressed, andI had to do something to make our lives better. I got a job working as a certified nursing assistant and worked fourteen days straight sixteen hour shifts. I found a two-bedroom one bathroom home because I needed my kids to have a home before Christmas. My husband didn't contribute much towards the move, it was all on me. in retrospect, I should've left him right with his holy parents. I paid all the bills in our home but hey they say for better or worse right? Six months into the marriage I started noticing she-male porn popping up on my computer and that was strange. I went to have a discussion with my husband about the disturbing content flooding my computer. It was hard for me to have this conversation with the man I love and took vows with, if he had an interest in men. I knew he had been to prison but damn could this man I have around my son really be into she-males. At that point I had to put it on the table, he denied it and indicated that it pops up when he watches porn. Months went by with no incidents of the she-male porn surfacing on my computer. One Saturday afternoon I was cleaning the house and I stumbled across something interesting. An SD card was lying on the floor of our bedroom closet floor. I promptly inserted it in my phone only to discover she-males having sex with men. I was angry, hurt, confused and wanting an immediate explanation. The man I had married harbored some secrets that could destroy his reputation and it damn sure* destroyed our marriage. It was time to confront him about this she-male porn. I had solid proof but he still tried to make excuses when we talked. Late that night I decided it was time to let the cat out of the bag, my blood was boiling already. My heart was pounding like crazy, that's when I asked him if he liked balls, I wanted to know why he would marry me knowing I'm not what he wants. He got so mad when I confronted him, but only because his homeboy was in the next room. That's when he just started fighting me, a punch to the mouth, I put my hand to my mouth and there was blood. I s aid to myself, hell no, I have to get out of there with my kids. His homeboy came into the living room to try to break up the fight between us and I broke free to get into my car with the kids. He came to the car and banged on the windows yelling obscenities and threatening me regarding telling others. I cannot believe that I married someone who is into she-males. I had given up everything in Georgia trusting him. I had to call the police and my my dad to intervene; they all arrived at the same time and my she-male loving husband ran off right before they pulled up. The officer asked me what made him go off and I explained that I had confronted him about the she-male porn he was watching. When my dad learned that he had punched me he said that I should have ran him over. Later my phone rung off the hook, to no surprise it was my sorry excuse of a husband crying and apologizing for everything. He requested that I didn't mention the reason why we were fighting to anyone.

*I later learned that his parents blamed me for their son's twisted feelings.. It was time for me to leave, and let the marriage go because I did not want to live with the "what if." I decided to relocate back to Georgia to get my life back on track and leave all the hurt, pain and anger behind me. When I left Maryland I thought it was the end of our communication, but he started calling me because I knew his dark scandalous secret. Over two weeks of him harassing me went by before the phone calls stopped and I was able to move on. I dodged a bullet and I never looked back.*

# HEARTACHE

*Have you ever met a guy and just fall head first into the shit. Well I have met a few of those in my life. There was a guy that I used to see at the gas station from my house from time to time and I had the biggest crush on him. He had the up north swag, I just had to have him to myself and now I know that I should have left his ass right there at that damn gas station store. We met up one-day in the park for the first time and several weeks later he moved in. You know in the beginning guys always seem to have their shine together, until slowly it starts fading. The amount of money he makes is decreases, he drops out of school, his car stops working and the neediness begins. It turns out he really wasn't who I thought he was and he turned out to be just like the rest. I should have known he wasn't right wearing that gas station jewelry. When I got into my fifth month of my pregnancy with his child he walked out on me and told me that he hopes my oldest child's father kills me. What decent person wishes death on the mother of their child? I went through hell with my pregnancy, the situation with him didn't make it any better and I felt like my family was treating me like* shit. I couldn't work because I was sick, depressed or even stressed out. The pregnancy took a toll on me mentally but God spoke to me and told me that I could handle it. There were days that I would just cry, have bad thoughts, thinking why me but I knew I had to be strong. I never imagined that I would have had to go through a pregnancy alone, it was a trying time. I remember going on the father of my unborn child's facebook page, he was talking shit about me and that crap would hurt to the core, especially after I had helped him. I had given him the down payment to get his car a few months prior, I had allowed him to move into our home and all I did was have his back, even when he worked a job paying him $7.50 per hour. I have never been a materialistic female, it has never been about money. I saw him weeks later at a nearby gas station, he didn't ask how we were doing. I'm just glad I believe in karma, it didn't take long for her ass to show up either. I got a phone call from him one late summer afternoon; he needed me to come get him from downtown Atlanta because his brakes went out and he had hit someone on a motorcycle. I intervened on his karma because he was the father of my child and I believed that I was obligated to be there for him. I believe that when people have karma coming to them it's best that you let it take its course, otherwise that person will never learn their lesson and they will continue with the same patterns.

With all the heartache, stress I ended up being admitted to the hospital, diagnosed with *preeclampsia six weeks early of my due date. I had gotten into an argument with my baby's father, and my stepdad, my blood pressure was sky high and I started having strong contractions. It was way too early for for my baby to be born, I hit the call bell to inform the nurse that I was having labor pains, this nurse told me I wasn't but I told her I know what contractions feel like. They proceeded to put me on the monitor, then gave me some medicine to stop the contractions but the medicine put me to sleep. I don't know how long I was out but I remember the nurse waking me up and informing me that they were preparing to take the baby, I said okay. I don't understand why I wasn't panicking at this point, I let her know that I have to pee and the nurse said go ahead. I walked into the bathroom and immediately blood just gushed out everywhere, it was like something you see in the movies. That's when the worry began, I remember them taking me into this cold room and preparing me for the emergency c-section. At this time my child's father entered the room, all I could do was lay there praying to God that my baby would come out fine. Once she was here I just started crying because she wasn't crying, I said God please and she let out a big cry. My heart didn't feel heavy anymore, she did have to stay in the hospital for a few days until she gained some weight and learned how to feed from the bottles. I was in the NICU every hour on the hour, I felt so bad that I allowed this to happen to my baby but I thanked God that he allowed me to give her life. Now my miracle baby is smart, beautiful and healthy. The father of my third child was very nasty with his words and that mess would really hurt my feelings. He was so stuck on social media women, at times I would question my looks and often ask myself am I beautiful in his eyes. My self-esteem was shot after dealing with him but deep down I still had a love for him. Certain moments his voice plays in my head from time to time saying to me that's why you got shot, I respect the person who shot you but I don't respect you. I will continue to be a mother to our child and to teach her not to ever settle for anything or anyone less than she deserves. a sucker like her dad. I don't regret anything I went through while carrying her because it was all worth it.*

# BREAKING POINT

*In May of 2016 I allowed my grandmother to take my oldest two to Maryland for summer vacation. As a mother, I try to protect my kids to the best of my ability and being I didn't have that when I was a child made me a pit-bull for mine. My one year old was leaving for Virginia a month later, I said hell I need a break but something didn't feel right in my spirit. My oldest daughter's father resides in Maryland as well, I didn't feel comfortable about her being with him but my grandmother wanted them to have a relationship without my approval. I kinda gave in at that moment, all of that changed once my son informed my grandmother that my daughter was on the verge of losing her virginity and at that sent me into mommy mode. The next day I planned to drive to Maryland to get my daughter because I didn't raise my child to give herself to no one but also to know her worth. As a young girl growing up I didn't have anyone to talk to me or teach me things of the world and that's why certain things happened to me. I vowed to be different when it came to my children but it wasn't happening to me. I packed up my car, with my youngest, and on only three hours of sleep I proceeded on my twelve hour drive to Maryland. When I got to North Carolina I picked up my daughters best friend because this happened around my daughters fourteenth birthday and even though I was disappointed in her, I still wanted to be supportive. I was really trying to get to her because I knew her father liked to put his hands on women and I didn't want him touching her, because I would have been in jail. Plus he was a known drug dealer I feared for my daughters safety every time she was with him and I would be damned if he ruined her life. I kept her away from that life and he wasn't about to expose her to anything else. When I got to her it was like a weight off my chest, thinking I can breathe now but we still had some conversing to do about the mistake that could've changed her life. I stayed for a couple of days to spend time with my family, then I had to get back on the road and I had to drop my baby girl off with her grandmother in Virginia for the summer. She was keeping her so I could work because I didn't have any support in Georgia, when it came to someone watching her while I worked. On my way back home I was really tired and it seemed like I wasn't ever going to make it home. I remember getting to Aikens, South Carolina getting out the car crying asking God to please let me make it home. My aunt got us a hotel room for the night. I thought that I just need some rest; I planned to get back on the highway in the morning. I took the girls to get some food, snacks for the night. We had planned to go swimming later that night. Suddenly my hands started feeling numb, my breathing started to get heavier and it was uncontrollable. I felt like* something was wrong, I told the girls to call downstairs to the receptionist and have her call 911. When the ambulance arrived I was sitting on the hotel's curb. I was trying to get it together because I saw how scared my daughter was for me but I couldn't control it. I was transported to the nearest hospital, they ran multiple tests but the result was I had my first anxiety attack. From that day on it changed my life, I had never heard of anxiety until that day. Ever since that day I have been fighting this thing and it hasn't been easy at all. I find myself not wanting to be alone because I think something bad will happen. At times I don't want to go to work, I don't like going out anywhere and this is a fight I battle with on a daily basis. I explained to a lady one day that I didn't want to go crazy and she said to me when a person goes crazy they don't think about going crazy. In other words I'm not going to go crazy but this has been a challenging battle for me. I fight everyday to leave the house, it has me really depressed at times, stressed out and exhausted. I have been to the hospital over twenty times thinking I'm having a heart attack in the last three years. I don't know what to do, I'm a strong person that has endured a lot of emotional, physical, and mental pain. I will not take any medicine for it because I don't want to be dependent on medication. I have actually started seeing a psychologist to get a better understanding of what is going on with me, maybe she can shed some light on why am I going through this and maybe conversing with her will heal some unhealed wounds. I have pushed people away because of this disorder that I have developed, I just *pray that one day it will go away and it will be just another testimony for me to share. I know one thing I won't ever give up because God didn't build me that way. I'm a fighter, I always have been and this disorder doesn't define me.*

# HEALING

*Life comes with everyday obstacles and best believe I have had my share of them in my life. Things haven't been easy being a single mother and a father to my son. I struggle everyday to find my purpose in this cold world and I haven't always been the perfect person throughout my life. Some things I had to find out the hard way, there were things I didn't have to go through to know that's not what I wanted for me or my kids. It's hard when you go through life feeling alone but I had to realize I wasn't never alone. God has protected me from a whole list of things but he does have you experience life lessons to make you a stronger person. It's been plenty of days I have cried silently asking why me. The relationship with my mother has become stronger, something I always needed and some relationships aren't meant to be repaired. Even though my grandmother did some things unexplainable she has had my back in other situations throughout my journey. I have some family members that don't agree with the financial help she extends to me. I'm at this point in my healing and it is a must, in order for me to live a healthy life. I had to forgive the people that hurt me for me and I had to ask God for forgiveness as well for the people I have hurt. There were chapters I needed to close in my life to allow my heart to heal and I had to be by myself in order for that to happen. Someone told me one day God gives his toughest battles to his strongest people, there are plenty of strong people but it's the ones that can endure who survive the battles. Life is a learning experience either you conqueror it or fold; but time won't wait for me. I had to know my self worth and stop giving myself to people that don't deserve the person I am. As the new year 2020 has arrived I have put some plans into play, this is my year. I've been holding myself back from my own success, and it's time for me to shine. At the end of the year I decided to write down everything that has to stop my growth in the past years and I set it in flames. It's time for me to be the woman God designed me to be, it will not be easy but I'm ready for the challenge. It's time for me to spread my wings and be the butterfly God has created me to be. I took some time off from relationships to focus on my children and making myself better. I keep giving myself to people that don't deserve it! Healing is the main key of having a healthy mind, body and soul. I refuse to become a human rocking chair!*

# AFTERWORD

*Starve the distractions of the world & feed your focus of achievement*

# ABOUT THE AUTHOR

## Te'ann Peaker

Te'Ann Peaker is a Georgian mother of three and a Maryland native. Her journey is one of a torrid tales, tough breaks and critical decisions on the pathway to destiny. She is transparent and passionate about combatting domestic abuse. Te'Ann currently works in the medical and pharmaceutical field while pursing other ventures.

Made in the USA
Columbia, SC
27 October 2024

44791764R10037